For my family – SB

*Acknowledging the work of Sea Shepherd
and all those who battle powerful forces to protect
and defend the vulnerable* – JT

Storm Whale

Sarah Brennan *illustrated by* Jane Tanner

Old Barn Books

Bleak was the day and the wind whipped down
When I and my sisters walked to town.

And the seabirds wheeled and the salt sea spray
Made dots and dashes, black and grey,
On the cold round rocks on the jetty's side
And the promenade where the children ride
On Shetland ponies, small and strong,
When the summer days stretch on and on.

And we held our hats as the cold wind blew
Through the grassy dunes as our wide skirts flew,
And we shouted out till our lungs were numb
But the buffets rendered our voices dumb.

Bright cheeks streamed like a rainy day,
White breath steamed and was hurled away,
Hair flew wild like a pony's tail...

And there, on the beach, lay the stranded whale.

Scarred old mariner, beached in hell,
Far from the cradling ocean swell,
Far from the peace of the ocean deep
Where ancient fugitives find their sleep.
Swept by the tide to its farthest reach,
Left with the kelp on the hard wet beach...

Dark as a demon, dull of eye,
Waiting in silence to drift...or die.

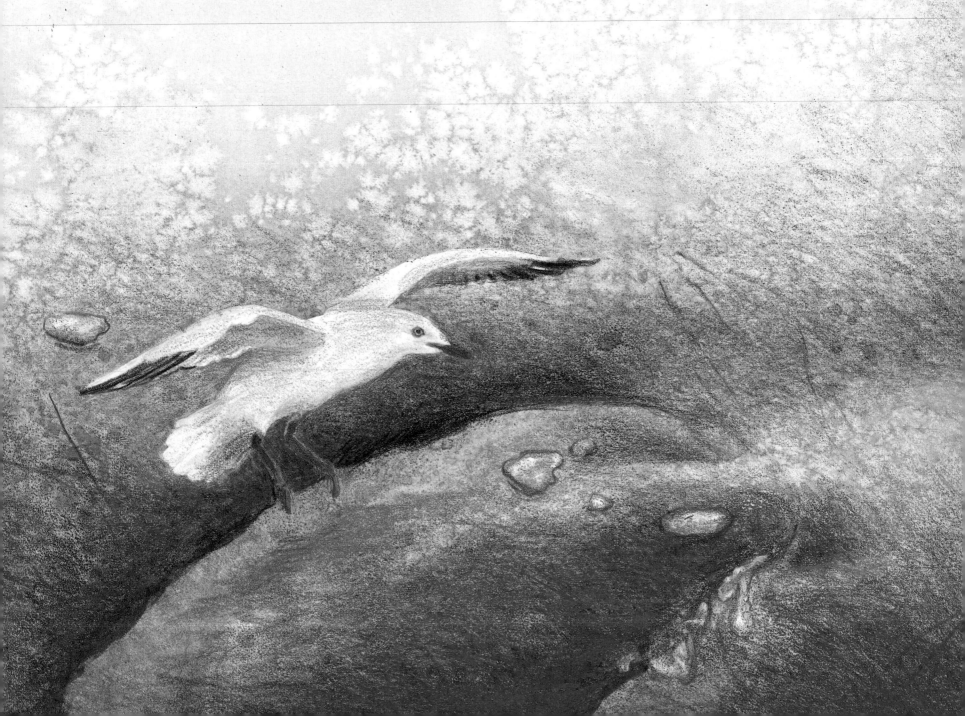

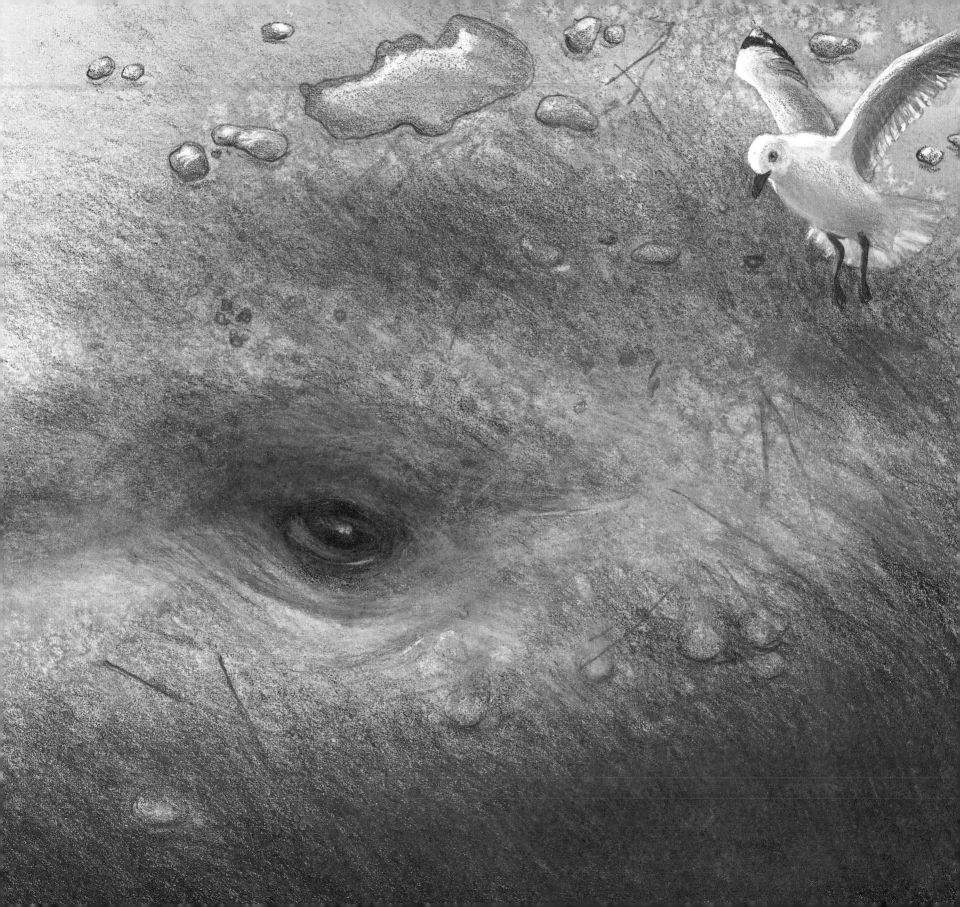

Long cold hours did we spend that day,
Down on the beach where the great beast lay,
Bending, bucketing pail on pail,
Lugging in vain at its listless tail...

Casting prayers to the wild wet air,
Which wouldn't listen and couldn't care.

Dusk rolled down with the driving rain,
Seabirds gathered to stake their claim.
Broken-hearted we hastened back
Home to our rented seaside shack.

Hugs at bedtime and fireside light,
But no one slept on that storm-filled night.

Tossed by tempest and torn by gale,
Our dreams lay lost
With the lonely whale...

Morning rose like a golden peach,
Glowing over the wide white beach.
Fair was the day and the sea becalmed,
And the sun shone soft like a healing balm.

There on the beach lay wrack and wreck
Wrung from the sea; the waves slip-slapped
Around old bottles, blue and green,
And shells, the strangest we'd ever seen,
And fishing nets, and planks and bones,
And seaweed, high as a mermaid's throne…

And there on the beach, on the golden shale,
Was not one sign of the stranded whale.

Scarred old mariner, safe from hell,
Back in the cradling ocean swell,
Back in the peace of the ocean deep
Where ancient fugitives find their sleep

Swept by the storm back out to sea
Where the harried and hunted-for...swim free.

Grand was the day and the sun shone down
When I and my sisters walked to town.

SARAH BRENNAN grew up on the slopes of Mount Wellington in Tasmania, reading under her bed
the washing up, writing lots of stories and poems, playing the bagpipes, exploring the bush and caring
of exotic animals. After studying law in Queensland, her varied career included bagging flour on a fact
line, fielding phones in a psychiatric hospital and typing letters (very badly), before settling down as a
in London for ten years. After moving to Hong Kong in 1998, she followed her childhood dream, beco
loved author of the funny and educational *Chinese Calendar Tales* and the *Dirty Story* series for prima
kids. She has a French husband and two daughters, and lives in Hong Kong beside a nature reserv
Chinese border, visiting schools in Hong Kong, China, South East Asia and Australia on a regul

JANE TANNER has a fine art and teaching background and began illustrating picture books full-tim
She loves working for children and drawing their attention to the natural world in all its awe and wo
acclaimed illustrator of the best-selling picture books *There's a Sea in my Bedroom*, *Drac and the Gre*
The Fisherman and the Theefyspray, *Lucy's Cat and the Rainbow Birds* and *The Soldier's Gift*. She is
illustrator of *Playmates*, *Isabella's Secret*, *Ride with Me*, *Just Jack*, *Love from Grandma* and *Lily and*
She lives in Australia and has won or been shortlisted for many prestigious awards there, includin
Book of the Year Awards in the categories of Picture Book of the Year, Younger Readers and Early

AN OLD BARN BOOK

First published in Australia in 2017 by Allen & Unwin
This edition first published in 2017 by Old Barn Books Ltd
West Sussex, England, RH20 1JW
www.oldbarnbooks.com

Distributed in the UK by Bounce Sales & Marketing.

Copyright © Text, Sarah Brennan 2017
Copyright © Illustrations, Jane Tanner 2017

ISBN: 978-1-91064-625-0

Cover and text design by Sandra Nobes
Set in Sabon by Sandra Nobes
Printed in China
1 3 5 7 9 10 8 6 4 2

Grand was the day and the sun shone down
When I and my sisters walked to town.

SARAH BRENNAN grew up on the slopes of Mount Wellington in Tasmania, reading under her bed to avoid the washing up, writing lots of stories and poems, playing the bagpipes, exploring the bush and caring for a menagerie of exotic animals. After studying law in Queensland, her varied career included bagging flour on a factory production line, fielding phones in a psychiatric hospital and typing letters (very badly), before settling down as a medical lawyer in London for ten years. After moving to Hong Kong in 1998, she followed her childhood dream, becoming the much-loved author of the funny and educational *Chinese Calendar Tales* and the *Dirty Story* series for primary school aged kids. She has a French husband and two daughters, and lives in Hong Kong beside a nature reserve near the Chinese border, visiting schools in Hong Kong, China, South East Asia and Australia on a regular basis.

JANE TANNER has a fine art and teaching background and began illustrating picture books full-time in 1984. She loves working for children and drawing their attention to the natural world in all its awe and wonder. She is the acclaimed illustrator of the best-selling picture books *There's a Sea in my Bedroom*, *Drac and the Gremlin*, *The Wolf*, *The Fisherman and the Theefyspray*, *Lucy's Cat and the Rainbow Birds* and *The Soldier's Gift*. She is the author and illustrator of *Playmates*, *Isabella's Secret*, *Ride with Me*, *Just Jack*, *Love from Grandma* and *Lily and the Fairy House*. She lives in Australia and has won or been shortlisted for many prestigious awards there, including the CBCA Book of the Year Awards in the categories of Picture Book of the Year, Younger Readers and Early Childhood.

AN OLD BARN BOOK

First published in Australia in 2017 by Allen & Unwin
This edition first published in 2017 by Old Barn Books Ltd
West Sussex, England, RH20 1JW
www.oldbarnbooks.com

Distributed in the UK by Bounce Sales & Marketing.

ISBN: 978-1-91064-625-0

Cover and text design by Sandra Nobes
Set in Sabon by Sandra Nobes
Printed in China
1 3 5 7 9 10 8 6 4 2

Old Barn
Books